Miffy's Adventures Big and Small

Miffy at the Library

Based on the work of **Dick Bruna**
Story written by **Maggie Testa**

Ready-to-Read

Simon Spotlight
New York London Toronto Sydney New Delhi

SIMON SPOTLIGHT
An imprint of Simon & Schuster Children's Publishing Division
1230 Avenue of the Americas, New York, New York 10020
This Simon Spotlight edition January 2017
Published in 2017 by Simon & Schuster, Inc.
Publication licensed by Mercis Publishing bv, Amsterdam.
Stories and images are based on the work of Dick Bruna.
'Miffy and Friends' © copyright Mercis Media bv, all rights reserved. Story adapted by Maggie Testa.
All rights reserved, including the right of reproduction in whole or in part in any form.
SIMON SPOTLIGHT, READY-TO-READ, and colophon are registered trademarks of Simon & Schuster, Inc.
For information about special discounts for bulk purchases, please contact
Simon & Schuster Special Sales at 1-866-506-1949 or business@simonandschuster.com.
The Simon & Schuster Speakers Bureau can bring authors to your live event. For more information or to
book an event contact the Simon & Schuster Speakers Bureau at 1-866-248-3049 or visit our
website at www.simonspeakers.com.
Manufactured in the United States of America 1216 LAK
10 9 8 7 6 5 4 3 2 1
ISBN 978-1-4814-6932-6 (hc)
ISBN 978-1-4814-6931-9 (pbk)
ISBN 978-1-4814-6933-3 (eBook)

Miffy and Grunty are
going to the library.

Aunt Alice is helping out
at the library.
Hi, Aunt Alice!

Aunt Alice stamps a
book.

Miffy wants to help.

Miffy stamps a book.
Miffy and Grunty want
to help some more.

They can help Aunt Alice
put away books.

Oh no!

Aunt Alice has
more books to stamp!

Miffy and Grunty can
put away the books
all by themselves.

"The covers will show
you where to put them,"
says Aunt Alice.

Miffy and Grunty

go to the shelves.

Grunty holds up
a yellow book.
There are stars
on the cover.

"That means it goes
up high like the stars,"
says Miffy.

Miffy holds up
a blue book.
There are flowers
on the cover.

"It must go next to
that flower!"
says Miffy.

Grunty holds up

a red book.

There is a
swimming bunny
on the cover.

Grunty sees fish swimming.
"Wait!" says Miffy.

A book cannot go
in a fish tank!

Hi, Aunt Alice!

"The **color** of the cover
shows you where to put
each book," she says.

Miffy places a red book
with the other
red books.

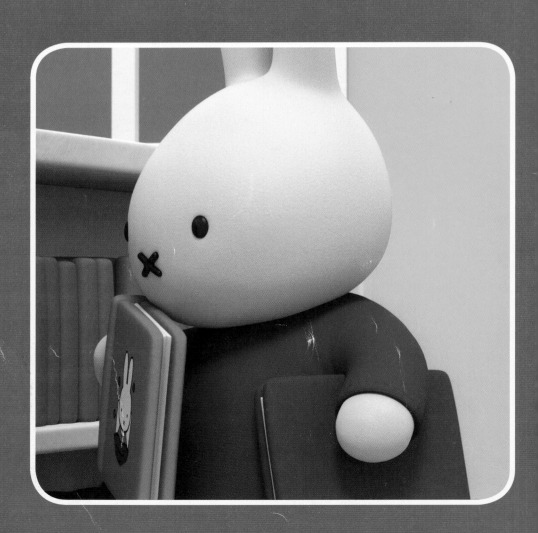

Miffy places a green book
with the other
green books.

Aunt Alice places
a blue book with
the other blue books.

All done!

Now Miffy picks out
books to read.

What a fun day
at the library!